A woman is a poem

—Khalil Gibran

Also by Christopher de Vinck

Rumors About God *(Silver Bow)*
The Voice Of A Confident Woman *(Silver Bow)*
Poems in Celebration of the *Muse* *(Silver Bow)*
Ashes *(HarperCollins)*
Mr. Nicholas *(Paraclete Press)*
Augusta and Trab *(Macmillan)*
Songs of Innocence and Experience *(Viking)*
Only the Heart Knows How to Find Them *(Viking)*
Things that Matter Most *(Paraclete Press)*
The Center Will Hold *(Loyola Press)*
Moments of Grace *(Paulist Press)*
Finding Heaven *(Loyola Press)*
Compelled to Write to You *(The Upper Room)*
Nouwen Then: Personal Reflections of Henri Nouwen
(HarperCollins-Zondervan)
Love's Harvest *(Crossroad Books)*
The Book of Moonlight *(HarperCollins-Zondervan)*
Threads of Paradise. New York *(HarperCollins-Zondervan)*
Simple Wonders *(HarperCollins-Zondervan)*
Threads of Paradise *(HarperCollins-Zondervan)*
The Power of the Powerless *(Hodder) (Doubleday)*
(HarperCollins) (Crossroad Books)}

A Feminist's Manifesto

Christopher de Vinck

Silver Bow Publishing

Box 5 – 720 – 6th Street,
New Westminster, BC
V3C 3C5   CANADA

Title: A Feminist's Manifesto
Author: Christopher de Vinck
Copyright © 2025 Silver Bow Publishing
Cover: "Nude " by Rodin
Layout/Design: Candice James
ISBN: 9781774033 (print)
ISBN: 9781774033 (ebk)j

Library and Archives Canada Cataloguing in Publication
Library and Archives Canada Cataloguing in Publication
Title: A feminist's manifesto / Christopher de Vinck.
Names: De Vinck, Christopher, 1951- author.
Identifiers: Canadiana (print) 20250211815 | Canadiana (ebook) 20250215284 | ISBN 9781774033708 (softcover) | ISBN 9781774033715 (Kindle) Subjects: LCGFT: Poetry. Classification: LCC PS3554.E1165 F46 2025 | DDC 811/.54—dc23

Author's Note

As the artist Auguste Rodin wrote "Art is always sacred." When we mix beauty with earthly things we see, perhaps, a glimpse of heaven, or at least a moment on a Sunday afternoon when we feel a certain thrill with the aroma of lilacs, or when we embrace a lover, or when we find a poem that reveals who we are.

"The main thing," Rodin wrote "is to be moved, to love, to tremble, to live." In these poems, I wrote how the love of a woman moves me, and that the main thing in our lives is to love. As equal lovers close the space between them, they tremble, they live.

Many years ago when I visited the feminist poet May Sarton at her home in York, Maine, as she and I read poetry to each other on her couch, she looked at me and said. "You know, Chris, all my poems are love poems."

This is a book about the equality of love shared between men and women: love and beauty combined, love and the erotic combined, love and silence combined. This is a book of poems that celebrates the physical beauty of men and women with the ease of what is familiar and equal between them.

To blend Rodin's illustration of a woman (cover art) with poetry seems to me to be a valid way to express a longing for the illustrations of our physical selves to blend with our spiritual selves, especially when we find what stirs us towards love.

There is no greater force in human existence than the power of mutual love, mixed with equal and eager eroticism. There is no greater peace than the moment when lovers embrace and whisper good night at the end of a chaotic day as they sleep under a forgiving moon.

May these poems touch upon what is sacred inside you.

Christopher de Vinck
Spring 2025

Contents

Introduction

A Feminist's Manifesto

Then we shall see Woman, liberated
by this upheaval, lift all inhibitions.
Love will be. And in one spasm,
all tongues will be untied. —Vera Herold

I have finally learned to unravel my tongue,
To open my blouse and purge the world
From pretending my breasts
Are for men's excavations.

I lean into the flower. I am not a flower.
I cover my skin with mud and saliva
Not perfumes made from musk and crushed plants.

Do you want to know a woman?
Ask her to undress the books she is reading;
Ask her to take you to the caves and trees she admires.

I am not a cliché to undress. I am an innovation.
I am tired of being a routine under your hands.
I am tired of your lips grazing my lips
When all you want is your own final satisfaction.
Pay attention to the words that spill from my mouth
Not from your liquid panting.

What do you think a woman is
Cotton candy that melts in your mouth?
Taste me in all my flavors.
I am not clay for your potter's wheel.
I form my own shapes for a man's pleasure.

If you want to join me for dinner,
Bring me shells and poetry as an invitation.

PART 1

A FEMINIST'S WARNING

The greatest feminists have also been
***the greatest lovers.* — Erica Jong**

Do you notice how my skin moans
When I am bending to the willow of your body?
Do you know I am made of petals and not birch bark?
When you undress me, what do you see,
The color of flesh? Don't you see
Swans swimming up from my ankles to my breasts?
I ought to taste like honey at your lips.
Do you see my hair is made from silk and not straw?
When I am under you, do you think that
I will break like glass? I am made of soft fur
And a cushion of spring loam.
Yes, I am delicate, but I will swallow you
When you least expect it.

THE POET TO HIS MUSE

You reside in what I write. —Anonymous

For you I arrange words like lilacs,
The aroma to please you,
The spring blossoms to please you,
The weight of my pen lessened
As the ink drains from my body.
When you watch the birds,
Or hear the bark of a dog,
Know you are in the neighborhood
Of my poems waiting for your arrival.
I place the book of my body
In your hands for your reading.
I am less sorrowful when you
Read my words aloud.
Your kiss tells me you want to
Take my book under your arm
And carry me to
The home of your breathing.
My book is my kingdom:
Love and sorrow combined,
Love when you open my cover,
Sorrow when my poems do not satisfy.
Do you keep vigil of my story?
Remember you are
Illuminated in each poem
For your nourishment?
I do not give you ashes
But the dry wood and fire of my poems.
My book is like the moon in your hand:
Light in the darkness during my dreaming.
I give you my robust self in what I write
Hoping these words will caress you,
And my love will feel less like a foreigner
And more like the citizen
Traveling on your breasts.
I am not a tourist. You are home.

THE FAIRYTALE OF
THE SWAN AND THE PRINCE

With each infusion I am renamed.-—-Anonymous

Do you know who I was last night
As I introduced my breasts to your lips?
You knew my name, but my name changed
When you unbuttoned my blouse
And you exposed my body to your eyes.
I was half woman and half swan
Bulging upward from the spring pond
As I slid onto the surface of you
With my open wings and empty thighs.
There was a moment in the water of our room.
The egrets gave us privacy.
I heard the cicadas in the darkness,
Or was that you etching
My new name onto your lips?
A woman is divided under a man:
Half flesh and half feathers.
This morning when you stroked my neck
And kissed my breasts
I felt as if I just returned from
The lake refreshed, renewed
With my name intact
Until tonight again when
I join once more the egrets and cicadas,
Baptized again with the
Moisture of your lips
And with the infusion of your white
Potion that transforms me again
Into a swan.

I'D LIKE TO DANCE WITH YOU
FOR ETERNITY

*What lingers is a hint of heaven.—***Anonymous**

When I die, what is left, a skull and teeth,
A network of bones?
What about my poems and
The memory of you at the beach
Under the blue umbrella?
Why does death have to be so complete?
Can we prepare a meal,
Rearrange our shelves for our books,
Plan a dance at the church hall.
Or even stall my dying until Tuesday?
What point is there
To place my body into the ground?
I need room to caress you in my dreams.
I need the space to dance
At the beginning with you again.
Please. We still need the room.
They say death lingers for a moment
And then we are forgotten.
Please remember, the dance is Tuesday.

FIRST SEX

The birth of a feminist. —**Anonymous**

No matter what I was told
I had to unfold the process myself.
Little did I know I would be asked
To unbutton his shirt
As he unbuttoned my dress.
I was told do be passive, to not participate,
To be submissive and be his pleasure.
When I felt his hand on my breast,
I was told to moan, or to pretend
That I was interested.
I did not expect the spike of bees
And the vibrations that
Streamed down between
My electric legs with such pleasure.
It was suggested that I give his genitals
Attention with my hands and lips.
I was interested in the curl of
His pubic hair and how
It felt coarse and pleasing
As I combed his black fur
Between my fingers.
I did not know how easy it would be
To stop being submissive,
And explore my body on his body,
To caress his chest with my breasts,
And to lick his neck.
I insisted that he place his hands
Behind his head as my hand massaged
The soft clay between his legs into granite.
I knew to use my hand as a pendulum,
And I was in control of the extraction.
That drained from his startled body.

WILD WISTERIA

We found a place, abandoned Eden perhaps.
There were traces of lions and swans,
Even trees and once a garden.
We found a place under the wild wisteria
As if the flowers were blue stars above us
And we sat and inhaled the aroma,
Or was that the aroma of your skin and breath
Weaving against me like waves of flowers?
This was our private place.
The grass removed the dew for us.
The sun covered our nudity with private shadows.
Before I caressed you, you leaned back into my arms
Asking that I touch your breasts with my tongue
To feel the waiting heat.
When you stretched your legs, you suggested
I think about an easy voyage
Between the waves of our private afternoon.
We were alone, in love, with the tailors in their shops,
And the widows in their churches,
And with the sparrows, the only intrusion.
Spring is made for the seclusion under the wild wisteria.

YOUR BREASTS

Your waist and your breasts, the doubled purple
of your nipples.—Pablo Neruda

The snow of my lips falls warm on your breasts.
The tide of your breasts roll onto my chest,
Like two shells with the tips of pearls.
I stretch my best length between your breasts.
There is space for the moonlight on your breasts,
A lesson I learned with my roving lips.
I harvest your breasts from the field of passion
With the scent of autumn blessed on your skin.
I watch as you shake off the loneliness from your breasts
And turn your breasts into flowers covered
With the dew of my anticipation. Oh that I could be the sun
And lick the dew from your petals each dawn.
Your breasts are never idle in my eyes,
Never silent in the shifting waves of my hands.
Your breasts have the substance of dough and laughter,
A cluster like two roses scented like flowers.
Your breasts do not sing about death.
Each time I find the shapes under my palms,
I feel the pulse of your desire and calm.
I touch the tip of each breast with the compass of my tongue,
The needle always pointing north to the pole of your beauty.
You are naked enough for my tired mouth revised
With the taste of your breasts, with the milk of your song
Spilling into my mouth, your breasts my nourishment,
Your breasts my poem.

I HAVE LIVED TOO LONG
WITHOUT THE SONG OF YOU

We sing to easy love and to hard singing.
— Anonymous

I have lived too long without the song of you.
I recognized notes in the throats of sparrows
And the way the trains moaned
Beyond the trees and in my dreaming.
I was easily mocked and checked for hearing loss,
But there was always movement in the air,
The sound of a caress, the music,
An aria, a sonnet, any sort of song
That I new was not just the empty air.
At first I was betrayed, the sound of tigers
Mimicking the disturbance I heard in the night,
The horizon bending, quicksand trying to swallow
Me and silence me and fill my mouth with sorrow.
I once said I heard a lullaby spoken from
The lisp of stars. I said I once heard
The pads of bears among the raspberry bush.
I tried to cover my ears with just the memory of you.
I tried to be deaf to your singing. I lost the argument.
I tried to kiss the song at the side of the swan's neck.
Even the moon sang a melody on the lake
Tilting the rhythm of water at the edge of the beach.
I kissed again the sound that I heard was not
Flutes or violins, but the song that I remembered:
The simple hum of your breathing.

THERE IS NO WAY TO STALK YOU HONESTLY

Love is less savage and more
The raw mouth kissing with fierce gratitude.
                        — Anonymous

There is no easy way to stalk you honestly.
I need to see you in your flowered dress,
And gather wild flowers for your hair,
And place my kisses at your feet.
My greed for you is more than hunger.
I am transformed from a beast to a man
With a poem in my hand.
I thought I'd prowl inside your dreams
And write words that make you sound
Like flowers or milk or the movement of your lips.
I assure you there is a softness in my dreaming
And a crude hunt in my seeking ways
To advance to your dancing.
I feel the thorns as I run towards you.
I even ignore the sharp stones under my feet.
The moon is my guide and the sun the thought
That illuminates your smile when I find you.
I thought at first the way to love
Was to ransack you with passion,
But love is less savage and more
The raw mouth kissing with fierce gratitude.
You are not bait for my hunger,
Not a shadow to cover my longing.
This is not an ambush but a greeting.

SOUVENIR

I grow old ... I grow old ...
I shall wear the bottoms of my trousers rolled.
                              —T.S. Eliot

I could easily abandon the poems,
Sell them as plums or cherry blossoms,
Count the coins in my pocket,
And buy a one way ticket to Paris.

In Paris I could sleep with a tourist,
Collect postcards together,
Toss coins in the fountains
At the Tuiletries Garden.

But I am a coward.
If I left the poems what would I do
With the history of my words
That I learned with my lips?
I am too old to learn a new language,
To image lilacs all over again,
To abandon the old regret:
The scars on my face
That identifies who I am.

It is easier to eat fresh plums
And admire each cherry blossom.

There is no woman in Pairs
Waiting for me to slip
Into the Seine of her body,
Or to mingle our colors in postcards.
I have no more coins to spend
In the Parisian gardens.
All I have left are my fading poems.

PART 2

A FEMINIST EXPLAINS TO A MAN
HOW SHE INTENDS TO SEDUCE HIM

The greatest feminists have also been
the greatest lovers. I'm thinking not only
of Mary Wollstonecraft and her daughter
Mary Shelley, but of Anais Nin,
Edna St. Vincent Millay, and of course Sappho

—-Erica Jong

I am not a monstrous love.
I will not devour you with my mouth and throat.

Perhaps I will use scissors and
Cut your hair to make you more vulnerable.
My fingers might play the piano of your skin.

I will offer you my phosphorus breasts
In the dark for your pleasure,
But I am not a savage with fire in my breath.
I have more habits for tenderness.

Yes, I enjoy the lantern of your phallus.
My mouth can be the eye on your chest.
I can corral clouds and slather you
With the falling mist of my body.

My strange hands might puzzle you at first.
They are not claws but they are aggressive.
When I touch the stones of your body,
You might feel a melting sensation.

You might think my tongue is a
Boat on your skin as you feel
The trawling nets of my fingers.

Touch me and you will see I am a tame star
With soft points and smooth edges.

My womb will welcome you with little violence.
I will not harm your erect flower.

Your nectar and my nectar will mingle
To create a turbulent sea.

We will bob like dolphins gulping for air,
Bathe in the saltwater of our bodies.

You might feel slight pain as I bite your shoulder.
I will ask you to undress me violently.

I will not pretend I am the sparrow and you are the hawk.
I will use my talons to pierce your flesh.
I am the tropical night. My humidity will exhaust you.
When we are through, I will watch you pant
And lean back as I swallow the souvenir of your savagery,
And I will maintain my frenzy and laughter.

TOURISTS TONIGHT

You lay beside me; your hand moved over my face
as though you had felt it also —
you must have known, then, how I wanted you.
— Louise Gluck

Even before I knew my hand on your breast,
I felt April on your skin, inhaled the fading winter air
As you witnessed the ritual of the waking bear.

Help me live a new season.
Help me retrieve the seeds in my dry pod.
We can find moisture together,
To encourage the growth of roots,
To witness the immersion of ourselves
Into the soil of each other.

I am not afraid to use the word erotic.
Stones are erotic.
The shadows of trees are erotic.
The salamander is erotic.

We have the wrong idea
About the tips of our fingers.
Touch defines the communication
Between us: a first caress
Is an invitation; a second caress
Suggests an undressing.
The third caress and I cannot tell
If it is your hand or my hand.

The country of your body, Spain perhaps,
Wears braids of wild flowers in your hair
And the stains of men from the arena.

I visit you this evening
With bowls of kisses from my mouth.
Let me feed you the taste of dusk.
Will you approve my passport
As I cross the border of your eagerness,

As I join you at the ridge where the
Earth and sea meet?

Let us become tourists tonight
Gathering souvenirs.

SONG OF THE ATHEIST

What do you seek--God?
you ask with a smile. —Walker Percy

What do I care that I do not love?
What difference does it make
That the trees are vertical
And not horizontal?
Love is a trifle, a worn penny.
Love stains the flowers and
Upsets the rotation of the moon,
So why bother with the night's violin
In some distant café in Paris?
I know a kiss: lips
And bits of skin and saliva.
I caress breasts, the plump flesh.
I even explored women
Between their legs: a pleasing spot
For a body's connection
And for a passing habit.
But love? My books feel better
In my hands. The deserts will still suck
The moisture from the sand if I do not love.
The constellations will not
Rearrange themselves in a new order.
What do I lose if I do not love,
Tangled dreams? Mud on my shoes
From the garden? A shared bed?
I do not need love. I have my own hands;
I have my own garden of lilies.
God is not in my seeds.

THE SEARCH FOR A
LASTING RESIDUE

Write as if your words are granite.
                    —-Anonymous

I seek immortality until dawn,
Roam the slick seams of night
Where the moon
Resides on her off cycle.

I seek a way to publish my body
Among the stars,
To be a new constellation.
I'd like to be a horse or a salamander.
I want my way
Of looking at the darkness to survive.

I'd like to understand
The phosphoresce of moist wood.
I'd like to live among the owls and fox
And exchange fur and feathers.
I'd take the risk to become the owl
Or the fox.

I wander at the base of the moon.
I lick the edges and touch the night air
As if the night can respond.

I can only address the stones in the garden,
Admit there is more beauty in a river
Then in all we imagine for each other.

I pick floating seeds in April
And wish to return the seeds
To the beginning.

I live among broken things:
The crack in the window,
The letters I have not written,
Even the way the flowers lean
For a moment before dying.

FEMALE; MALE

Notice the difference, of course.
— **Anonymous**

Notice the difference:
One body is made of soft lava
And the suspended waves of the sea.
There are spheres and summits,
Even a delicious moist valley.

The other body has more lines
And flatlands except for
The protruding rock
That is made from an expanded root
Stored with liquid.

They both have form and purpose.
They both have muscles and skin.
They are the same species and enjoy
The comfort of their bed,

But both are also made of nectar
And when they mingle
In the mouths of bees and desire
They make sweet honey.

THE SPRING A WOMAN NOTICED

Yes, I deserve a spring —Virginia Woolf

I did not notice the sparrows at the feeder,
Or the arrival of daffodils in the garden.
They say the warm air has arrived from the south
And the soil is moist again for dormant seeds.
I did not feel the new heat, or hear the roots moving.
I was told the light is longer in the afternoon,
And the violent stars arranged themselves
In their new positions.

But when you arrived and kissed me,
I felt the sparrows of your tongue on my breasts,
And your flower extended inside my garden.
I noticed the heat of your skin against my skin,
And how malleable the soil of your legs felt
During the movement of your root
Inside the length of my new light.
At night, when we were through
With our love making, I saw out our window
The stars. I noticed their calm stillness.

AMONG THE TREES AT DUSK

A vastness of pines, murmur of waves breaking,
slow play of light, solitary bell,
twilight falling in your eyes, toy doll,
earth-shell in whom the earth sings!
— Pablo Neruda

As we walked among the pines
In the closing part of the day,
There was a new seduction
Among the trees,
Not just the aroma of the trees
But the sudden fragrance
From your body,
A sudden aura perhaps
From within your breasts
Or under my skin.
There was the sudden darkness
As the sun no longer found
The opening among the trees
And we felt a new privacy.
I liked how you asked me without words
To undress you as you guided
My hand to your buttons
And brushed aside the cloth of dusk
From your breasts.
When you said you wanted to extract
The pine sap from my body,
I too undressed as you watched
My bough extend from my trunk
As you spread the pine needles
Of your body as a bed on the ground
And we became forest savages,
Beasts at least, perhaps even lovers.

A WOMAN'S BREASTS

I liked him because
I saw he understood or felt
what a woman is —-James Joyce

Part of the whole,
Filled with milk at times,
And lust at other times,
Formed in the shape of dunes
And the tips of
Black-eyed-Susans.
They are good for pleasure
And for the movement
Of tongues,
And for the ease of lips
And for comfort.
Buttons are their enemies,
Hands their playthings,
Passports to adventure.
The first spark for a relief.
They are round and oval,
Moon shaped and pearls;
Hives filled with honey
And always
Unapologetically alive.

THE CARESS OF THE SEA

That's the thing about sex in the sea,
it is once utterly foreign, yet there are
hints of the familiar---but only just.
      —Marah J. Hardt (Marine Biologist)

There is no difference between
The caress of the sea and my greeting you
In my room this afternoon.
My bed is still water.
Salt and shells are in suspension;
The tides of my blanket paused.
Even the gull of light is silent,
But when you arrive
And the beach sand feels
The movement of your body approaching,
The ocean water rolls on its back
Hoping for your touch.
My bed begins to curl open.
We taste bits of salt on our lips.
I watch you step out of the shell
Of your dress as the tides
Of my blanket float you
Nude to my side as the gull's light
Illuminates your breasts
And we can no longer tell the difference
Between the movement of the ocean
And the movement of our bodies
Spawning like bluefish gulping for air.

I AM A WOMAN ... I KNOW WHAT I WANT

To do something quite common,
in my own way. — **Adrienne Rich**

Do something common.
Say my name or unbutton my blouse.
Tell me how you plan to enter my body.
You cannot regulate the valves of my breasts,
Or manipulate the flow between my legs.
I can adjust my mechanical hand
And control your breathing.

Place your ear on my chest.
Do you hear the sobbing?
I too want the movement of your tongue
In my mouth pacing my heartbeat.

I ache for you to go hard. Please.
I am not confined to your desires.
I have my own adjustments.
Drink for a moment between my breasts.
Seek the shells and pearls hidden there.

Let me grope for who I am
On the surface of your skin.

I'd like to move with you, the way seagrass
Moves, a swaying together,
Feeling the currents of our hands,
Knowing the tide will come when the moon
Licks the surface of our bodies,
Rolling us towards the dry sand.

I am not afraid to feel your roots
Extending into my soil,
Seeking moisture for your veins.

I place modesty on the shelf and spill my books
Onto your chest as I open page after page
Of passion, dressing you with new skin.

I am thirsty. Open my faucet.
Release the pressure. Let me feel how you
Gush into me. Bring your wet tongue.
Caress my throat, but then
Satisfy the lower dryness deep inside
My hidden self. Find me there
Rich with sudden moisture
As I close my walls around you,
The way ordinary people do.

PART 3

UNDER MY DRESS

Under my dress blazed a field of flowers
        -—-Alejandra Piscarik

Under my dress, the length of the Nile.
Under my dress the taste of saffron.
Under my dress ocean currents.
Under my dress almonds and pomegranates.
Under my dress dunes and cherries.
Under my dress the skin of the Sahara.
Under my dress, taffy and salt.
Under my dress clams and flamingoes.
Under my dress, a nest of fur.
Under my dress buds of lilacs.
Under my dress moonlight and Venus.
Under my dress, seek who I am.

EXPERIMENT WITH YOUR BODIES

Who ever desired each other as we do?
— **Pablo Neruda**

They say there is nothing we do
That has not already been done.
Do they kiss as we kiss with the
Pulp of oranges in their mouths?
Does the man examine
The woman's breasts as if they are eggs
In the nest of his hands?
Do they make love on an ordinary bed,
On an ordinary beach of dry sand?
We could tell them about
Riding on the backs of whales
And how we nearly drown
In ecstasy each time.
Does the man know how to roll
A woman's breasts into sweet taffy?
Does the woman know how to
Pull the length of a man
Into a single spasm?
We could demonstrate what we do
When we undress, explain how
We walk at night
Among the herons at the lake
And measure our steps
Towards the flesh on each star.
We could give them seeds
And show them how to
Part the soil of their bodies
With hands made of wheat and lavender.
Let's tell them to experiment
With their bodies and feel the whale
Pulsing between them.

CARNAL APPLE

Violent or sweet, undress.
        —Anonymous

It does not have to be
Violent or sweet,
Bold or fresh.
It does not have to be
Nude or dressed,
Now or soon,
Evening or afternoon.
It may be breasts
One moment,
And tongues the next;
Giggles or moans,
But it is always sex.

WHERE ARE THE LILACS?

You are going to ask: and where are the lilacs?
                        — Pablo Neruda

If you ask where are the lilacs,
I will point to your breasts.
If you ask if I ever heard the bells of Madrid,
I will point to your thighs moving.
If you ask if I ever touched the skin of a gazelle,
I will caress your arms and legs.
If you ask about the last great book that I read,
I will opened the pages of your legs
And read aloud the sighs that you make.
If you ask about my relationship with women,
I tell you they all washed into the watercolor of you.
If you ask what I enjoy eating,
I will touch your lips with my tongue.
If you ask what is my favorite body of water,
Lake or sea, river or pond,
I will sway my hand inside your body
And say this is where I want to always swim.
I am the lilacs draped on your breasts.

A HUNTING MAN SPEAKS

Let me find you in the forest of my desire.
I will look under the rocks covered with moss.
I will taste the mushrooms and berries,
Wear ferns in my hair, consult the bears,
And ask them where they found honey.
The forest is dark, the leaves are the shadows
Of other women. I seek the aroma
Of pine sap on your palms. There are no flowers
In the forest. The light does not offer enough light.
When I touch the fur of the wolf, the wolf
Becomes a fawn. When I touch the fur of the fawn,
You lie back and spread your legs
And ask that I slowly enter your forest
With the flight and tip of my hunting arrow.

FOREPLAY SUGGESTIONS

*Licence my roving hands, and let them go
Before, behind, between, above, below.*
            — John Donne

Place your shoes under the bed.
Arrange your breasts
Between your open buttons.
I'll drape my shirt
On the back of the chair.
Rest your body beside my body.
We can form a wheel
When we begin to insert ourselves
Into the hub of our hips.
Let us form a circle with our skin,
Or we can rest at first
As ferns do in the moist shadows
And lean over each other.
Take the clip from you hair
And let your hair fall
On both sides of your breasts
As foam from Niagara.
Let me splash my tongue
On your nipples as you
Stroke the blossom
Between my legs in preparation
For the extraction of nectar.

A MODEL'S AGREEMENT

For me, a nude photograph should be erotic, not devoid of emotion.
The body is a sensual thing, sensuality being one of its most beautiful
and meaningful qualities. **— Wynn Bullock**

Fine. Look at me if you must, and the curtain behind me, and
The fronds of the tropical plant. What purpose?
To gaze with desire, to excite your body with the image of my body?
If that is all, take pleasure as you look at the tips of my breasts
And their symmetry. I will not look directly at you.
I will think about parrots or sand castles, I will distract myself,
And leave you to my body, to your private viewing.
I thought you might enjoy my arms lifted upward
To give my breasts the appearance of a universal shape:
Firm, moon-like, easy to make you think they are for your tongue.
See how I shift my pelvis to your left and
Make the curve of my waist more appealing?
I thought you would enjoy the hair at the intersection of my hips
And stomach. If you'd like to paint my figure on the easel of your mind
Feel free to wet the pointed brush of your body and slowly stroke
My image on your canvas.
If you are a photographer, set the camera of your memory
With a wide lens that will allow more light onto the film of your desire.
I will stand nude for a few more moments
To let you remember what I look like beside the tropical plants.

EVENING PLAN

Tie your heart at night to mine, love,
and both will defeat the darkness
                    — Pablo Neruda

I tie you to me not with
Ropes or lust but with the
Length of my arms and
With the strands
Of my legs and tongue.
I want to defeat the dark
And ignite the spark
Between us like a star
That penetrates the night.
I cross over you with
The eclipse of my hands,
Casting a shadow
On your breasts. I extend
The warm length of my sun
Easing into your valley.
Let us sew together
The fibers of our bodies
And create our own
Constellation in the galaxy
Of our room as the moon
Cradles us in subdued light
Until we untie
The ribbons of our skin
And unraveled the thread
Of our tongues before we sleep.

FIRST TIME

I discovered that your
Breasts were shaped like the moon
When I opened your dress
And you cleared the darkness
From my eyes.
You did not tell me your nipples
Were made from brown pearls,
And tasted like honey.
When you opened your legs
I found that I fit inside you
Better than a key, not mechanical,
More like a dolphin
Easily submerged in your
Foam and water.
Thank you for connecting
Your lips to my lips,
Flowers that mingled with the
Bees of our tongues
As we exchanged nectar.
When you lined the length of you
Against the length of me
Before we slept, I knew
We dissolved into the last space
That separated us.

I LOOK FOR YOU EVERYWHERE

I see your image, a bonfire,
burning in the water.
I searched, but no one else
had your rhythms.— **Pablo Neruda**

I look for you everywhere:
In the silk patterns
At a dress shop window,
On the surface of the lake,
The lily pads especially.
I look for you each time
The geese arrive,
And I look up for your
Breasts with wings.
When I taste an orange,
I seek your flesh
On my tongue,
The pulp especially.
When I look into
The fire at the hearth,
I see if the flames
Mimic your dancing.
I look for your face
In the face of a woman
Walking her dog.
When I touch
The tops of bushes
I think of your
Garden of Eden
Between your legs.
Dew? I think of you
Emerging from the shower.
A book? I think of
Caressing your spine
Before I open your pages.
You, especially.

PART 4

A WOMAN SPEAKS TO RODIN

A woman's naked form belongs to
no particular moment in history;
it is eternal, and can be looked upon
with joy by the people of all ages.
> — Auguste Rodin

Join me in my marble skin.
Polish my breast with your tongue.
I am the soft stone in the sun.
I throb under heat.
My mouth is eager for your
Chisel hidden inside your pocket.
We can forget about the moon.
Her light is tin, hard to retain,
Her shape when placed in the heat.
Your voice is a sweet hammer.
Turn the shape of my
Arms and thighs into a solid form.
When you are finished
Make me stand in the public
Of your eyes and know
It was a pleasure standing nude
For you to complete the sculpture
Of what I offer you each night.

I COULD CLAP TWO STONES TOGETHER

And I watch my words from a long way off.
They are more yours than mine. —Pablo Neruda

I could clap two stones together
So that you will hear me in the distance.
I tried waving my arms like the legs of a beetle,
But you did not look my way.
I thought about making a fire with my poems,
Igniting the idea of my lips on your breasts,
But then I thought you'd rather feel my hands
And not the acrid smoke of my melting passion.
I thought about borrowing the sparrow outside my window
And teach him how to sing your name,
Or at least to perch on your finger,
Spread open his feathers and mimic my desire
To undress and embrace you with my wings.
At best I send you this poem.
Notice my handwriting is uneven. It leaps
With each pulse of my heart when I think
Your eyes will caress each word
And I am not with you to read the lines aloud
Before I kiss you.

UNDRESSING

...as the dough rose,
doubling your breasts
---Pablo Neruda

The aroma
That rises
From your skin
As you undress
Suggests
The fragrance
Of an orange,
The scent of the
Jonquils undressing.
When you unfold
Your breasts,
Pearls are jealous,
Loaves of bread
Wish they too
Were made for
My hands
And mouth.

I LOVE YOU AS THE SIMPLE TASTE OF SALT

I love you without knowing how, or when,
or from where. I love you straightforwardly.
—Pablo Neruda

I love you as the simplest taste of salt,
And the spasm of sugar on my tongue.

I love you with my private obelisk,
With the hieroglyphs carved with your lips
From the base upward.

I love you as the moon bathes in sunlight,
And the ease of a door on oiled hinges.

I love you as the rose loves her fragrance,
As the color of clouds are exposed.

I love you as the promise that my hands
Were built for your breasts.

I love you without the need to explain
Bears or chariots floating among the stars.

I AM YOU

Perhaps not to be
is to be without
your being,
  ---Pablo Neruda

I exist
Because you exist.
When you breathe,
I breathe.
When you taste an orange,
My tongue
Lingers on the juice.
When you speak,
My lips move.
When you sleep,
I dream.
When you read,
Words caress my chest.
When you inhale
The aroma of spring,
The perfume of you
Splashes on my skin.
When you were born
My birth.

TO BE FOUND IS TO BE RECOGNIZED

And it was at that age... Poetry arrived
in search of me— **Pablo Neruda**

How did you find me?
Did you hear my crying
In the dark when my blanket
Was my only companion?

Did you touch my chest
With your fins
When I swam in the lake that summer?

I thought I felt the pollen
From your lips when I caressed a rose.

When I stood beside a wood fire,
I thought I saw you leap upward
Like a gypsy in red silk.

Was it you who tapped my window
During the storm?

Was it your voice and not
The nightingale?

Did you consult the map
On your skin and retrace the path
My hand took to your breasts
To find me?

I am glad you pushed the blanket aside.
I am glad the tip of your fin
Caressed my chest.

I am glad your pollen touched my lips.
I am glad it was you in the fire.

I am glad the rain on my window
Was your skin caressing the glass.

I am glad your voice mimicked
The nightingale.

I am glad you remembered
The path I took to your breasts.

I am glad that you found me
And remembered who I am.

LOVER'S ENTWINED

I am one, sir, that comes to tell you
your daughter and the Moor are now
making the beats with two backs.
        -—William Shakespeare, Othello

Let us close the space between us.
Let us merge as one stone, one grain of wheat.
Let us join our bodies and step into a single voice
As we split ourselves open to each other.
We are not two orbs colliding, more a wound
Tied to heal with no visible scar
Where we cannot tell where your breasts begin
And where my phallus ends
As we become a single body submerged
In the night's shadow as a writhing beast
Curled in the skin of our blanket
As we pant and die in mortal passion.

I UNDERSTAND YOU NEED TO BE ALONE
WHEN THE TIDE RECEDES FROM YOUR BODY

How much of love-making is perfunctory?— -Anonymous

I understand you need to be alone
When the tide recedes from your body,
When there is a cooing of doves
Out the window and time
Is forgotten in a book of poems,
Or inside the passion of a novel
That you are reading.
I am but a stone in the garden of your beauty,
A seed in your flower, perhaps even
A few words in your book.
I am an inconvenience. I understand
That you need to protect your solitude,
You need to rechristen your body
As your own after you give yourself to my body,
After you abandon a part of yourself
When you offer your breasts
And think about your book, when you
Offer your open legs and you'd
Rather be in the ocean alone among the
Foam and waves.
I understand that I take a part of you
During our love-making as I fold and refold
Your body and focus on the surface of your breasts
And not on your blood and milk.
When I enter you, your face becomes a new face:
Sometimes a mask, sometimes a shrug of acceptance.
I understand you need to recover alone from the duty of
Your open wound.

A NOTE TO EVE

I am not jealous
of what came before me.
        — Pablo Neruda

I do not need to know
How many men touched your hair,
Or unlaced your dress.
I do not need to know their names,
Or the amount of moisture
That they left on your lips.
I am not interested
In who came before me,
Adjusting your arms to their waists,
Aligning the height of your hips
With the height of their hips.
I do not need to know if anyone
Spilled poetry on your skin,
Or dragged the moon
And used it as a pillow for your head.
Do not tell me how many men
Used their tongues on your skin.
I do not need to know if they murmured
When they touched your breasts.
What was the flavors
Men injected inside you:
Cherry? Vanilla?
Men cream and loveliness?
No, I do not need to know.
You are Eve to all men.
I have no exclusive rights
To your fruit.
My name is not Adam. I am just
Another man waiting for my turn
To enter Eden.

WHEN YOU ENTER THE ROOM NUDE

The evening's threshold is rising. —René Char

When you enter the room nude,
I think of the passing moon
And the leaves of the willow.
I think of the way
The summer grapes are filled with
Summer juice.

When you enter the room nude,
I watch you walk as a heron
In the reeds, a bold Eve in the garden.

When you enter the room nude,
I spill the blanket from my legs
As our bed becomes the sea;
As you lean over and swim
Up the currents of my chest.

I taste the salt on your breasts
And you taste the salmon
Of my spawning as we float
On the sea foam passion for passion,
Our sea-flesh equally divided in our room.

PART 5

A WOMAN SHARES HER PREFERENCES

I like my body when it is with your
body. It is so quite new a thing.
> — e.e. cummings

I want this to be simple,
Nothing planned or mechanical,
My easy mouth on your easy mouth,
The local movement of our tongues,
Nothing exotic: cotton sheets not silk,
The aroma of spring, not incense.
I'd like to follow the path of your body,
Not a foreign terrain, or wide valleys,
Just your legs and thighs,
Just your chest with no detours.
Look how ordinary the sky. I want ordinary
Between my legs, no dragons,
No frantic salmon upstream,
Just your body easing into my body
As a rose stem breathing upward
Through the spring soil.
We can mimic the rain, not a storm,
Just the rain on the backs of leaves.
We do not have to devour the moon,
Or exchange loud moans and sighs,
Just simple words will do:
Love, touch, there.

SIMPLY

*What baffled him was that
there should be all this fuss
about something simple
as love.* — Gustave Flaubert

I am a primitive lover.
I can only bring you
Stones and beads,
Perhaps a bit of
Pollen on my cheek.
I can approach the side
Of your breast
And use my
Common tongue
To seduce you.
I have simple hands
To drape your skin
With patch work.
I have no flourish
Of feathers,
Or spasms of heat
To offer you, just a few
Ordinary strokes
Between your legs,
A kiss, my steady body
That can enter your body
On a normal evening.

MY BREAST ARE MEANT
FOR YOUR FIRE

Give yourself only in love.
            — Anonymous

I see your hand
Like a Japanese fan
Waving above the
Heat and blossoms
Of my breasts.
Let your lips
Mimic the tide
As your mouth
Washes over
The surface
Of my breasts
In rhythmic currents.
Please reside
Between my breasts.
Use the space to
Begin your caress.
Move from
The valley to
The brown tips
And ignited me
With fire and with
Your tongue.
I am made for this.

WE DIE EACH MOMENT OF LONELINESS

We commonly die to the affections
of those we see no more, and they to ours;
absence is the tomb of love. —Pierre Abélard

I will be impersonal. I will not mention my name.
You can read my face if you wish, even touch my arm
And see how I react, but I am a distant woods
Where there are no ferns or humidity.
I reside in the sustained tower of my swollen body.
I am an obstacle for your lips. I maintain my invisible earth.
You will not feel a tremor when I am beside you.
You might hear my surplus in your dreaming.
I live a soundless fate where you do not belong.
Everything is a few days from death.
Let me occur only in your sleeping. I want to be new
Each time you see me, but I hide the routines of my body.
I am endlessly dead without you.

YOU ARE THE ONLY CITY

Paris is a woman. —Jack Kerouac

As far as I know
Your body is already a dream,
Paris perhaps.
I have never been to Paris
But image what Paris must be
When I think of your breasts
And the Seine, and the linden trees
That cover the streets of your body
With what I imagine.
They say there are booksellers
Along the river, and the great cathedral
Bulges on all fours like a lion.
I think of myself
As the shadow under your fur.
I think I would like to read you
As a used book, a treasure I found in Paris.
There are poems about spring in Paris.
Does Paris know how you visit me
With the aroma of daffodils on your skin?
There are writers who lived in Paris
And kept their notebooks fresh
With the sound of dark nights:
A violin, women laughing in the streets.
Pairs is a collage in what I think.
At times I drink the café of your lips.
When I need relief I imagine
The Paris of you caressing
The cobblestones of my body.
Paris loans us the moon,
Suggests the moon is a woman
Illuminating the streets
When she walks between my legs.
To kiss Paris is to discover Paris;
To dream Paris is to write a poem.
Open your dress as I write
About the two cities:
The Paris of you and what I imagine.

WOMEN HAVE SECRETS IN THEIR BREASTS

The weight of jewels in your hand. —Anonymous

Unless you know what it feels like
To have a woman's breast in your hand,
You will never know the sounds of Paris,
Or the sighs of spring.
Women have secrets in their breasts,
Hidden powers they can give you
If you know how to use your hands
With tenderness. Women have
More than milk stored inside their breasts.
Poetry trickles down their throats when you drink.
You will feel slight spasms and hear murmurs
When you feel a woman's breast in your hand.

ONE NIGHT STAND

Sometimes sex is just about sex.
— Anonymous

I am made of buttons and threads.
My hair is silk; the curls between
My legs are jumbled twin.
The tips of my nipples are buttons,
The bulge at the joint of my thighs
An electric switch.

If you want to remember me,
Unbutton my blouse
And keep a thread from my dress
So that you will have evidence
You unraveled me.

I AM A WOMAN ABLE TO LOVE

I want to be simple legs spread,
hands glued to your hands
My mouth easy, my mind one color.
        — Rikki Ducornet

It is easy to spread my legs,
Even place them on your shoulders.
It is easy to be a spectacle
For your eyes, fruit for your
Hands and lips.
My mouth is easy; my body
Is flexible, able to accommodate
The length and pulse of your desire,
But there needs to be a perfect rising
Under the approach of your dew.
I am not a fragment of sunlight,
I am the full orb
Burning against the earth of you.
I can transform the serpent
Between your legs into a fern or salmon
With the right words from your lips.
If you devour the sun of my body,
There is only darkness.
Whisper your roots into my soil.

LET ME SPEAK TO YOU ABOUT LOVE

*Two people in love, alone, isolated from the world,
that's beautiful.* —Milan Kundera

Let me speak to you about love
At the edge of the butterfly's wing,
A delicate outline that mimics
Your breasts, a color
Gathered from the flowers.
Love is not just a moment's swoon
Or an attraction, love smooths
The sheets on the bed.
Love remembers the humidity
On our skin.
Love opens a window in July
And speaks about the sunrise.
If you want love, it is not enough
To unbutton your dress,
Or to reveal the slant of your breasts.
Love is the salt on your skin,
A moment's greeting.
Love is the ancient ritual:
Feathers in a sash,
The dance with bells around our ankles.
Love is a blessing on your forehead,
My tongue touching your lips,
The sound of the summer cicadas at night
When we are awake
Breathing beside each other.

MORNING POEM

*In ancient times it was an absolute rule that
after a night of lovemaking, the man had to produce
a poem and have it delivered to his love
before she awakened.* —Anaïs Nin

I took notes before I wrote this poem.
There were words that I found
Floating over your skin.
When you undressed I heard
Words that I did not understand,
But when you exhaled and I touched you,
There were sounds, ancient syllables,
Hints of a forgotten language,
Perhaps words used the first time
A woman tasted water,
Or the way the moon touched her face
And she felt a release.
When we moved against each other,
You held my shoulder and
Whispered the names of birds:
Peacock, sparrow, the heron
With its long beak.
When I entered you, you opened
As if you were a still lake.
You streamed over my skin.
You lapped onto the reed of my body.
When I touched your breasts,
You mimicked the movement
Of the tides on hot sand
And formed dunes against my chest.
There was a moment between
Our spasms and stillness,
A sudden expansion of wings
Yours and mine.
We were no longer ordinary lovers
But part beasts with surging tongues
And part flowers leaning into each other
Exchanging pollen and nectar,
And then the silence.

There is a Japanese tradition:
After lovemaking, the man
Writes a poem and leaves it
Beside the woman before she wakes.
When she reads the poem
She will know that her erotic self
Returned to her ordinary living.
I watched you in your dreaming.
I brushed a bit of hair from your face.
Did you hear the peacock in your sleep?

PART 6

WHAT YOU FEEL LIKE INSIDE ME

Everywhere in my dreams floats a feminine odor
Like an erotic sore with ultra fine needles.
            —-Joyce Mansour

I feel the prick of Eros and the lingering aroma.
There is a sudden shock, not exactly pain,
A slight injection. I recognized my own feminine odor,
But not the dryness of his breath.
I feel like a specimen on a cork board
With fine needles piercing my hands and legs.
The weight of his passion
Is a thick volume, pages of flesh
Leafing over my breasts.
There is no sound during the vaccination
Like waves at a waltz with no music,
But there is always the rhythm,
The pulsing inoculation.
I feel the extension each time,
Perhaps how an owl feels making its way
Upward inside the structure of a barn.

FLIGHT OF THE QUEEN BEE

To make yourself beautiful
you oiled your body with honey,
enchanting the bees. **—Velimir Khlebnikov**

I live with my appetite of desire,
A special madness hidden in the living wax
Between my thighs, seeking
Sunlight and the flesh of your petals.
I seek simple legs apart,
Breasts glued to my breasts,
A comfortable mouth at ease on my lips,
My mouth filled with your nectar,
Easy to taste and swallow.
Let me devour you as if
Drinking the moon-flower.
I am not a hidden dragon in the dark.
You illuminate my body.
I can see your blossom's flame extending
At the tip of your stem.
I wish to be the star
Between the earth and sun of your body.
Uncoil your arms and legs.
Let me lick the pollen from your skin.
My wings beat like bees with a purpose.
Let me form honeycombs inside you.

INSIDE THE WOMB

If my tongue could reach your womb
through your mouth —Ithell Colquhoun

If my tongue could reach into your mouth
And extend down your throat and enter your womb,
Would I learn a new language?
Would I taste Paris or the shell of a turtle?
If I could reach my hand inside our womb,
Would I feel sheep skin and smooth petals?
Would there be palm oil on my fingers?
What if I could step inside your womb
And look around, would there be drawers
Filled with bottles of perfume
Or with children's drawing: mice with big ears,
Trains or butterflies with dragon wings?
If I sit inside your womb, would there be silence?
Would I hear you breathing?
I would like to linger inside your womb,
Make myself comfortable,
Mix my liquid with your silk pool
And feel the pressure of your pulsing walls
Until, please, you birth me each night
In what you remember.

MINOTAUR

The poet is a long animal from infancy.
                    —-Luiza Neto Jorge

I was a hairless animal at birth,
Beneath my skin an unknown passion.
Children lean against the moonlight.
They believe trolls
Live inside the roots of trees.
When I became a man
My fur curled between my legs.
I felt a surge as if I owned
A stem with thorns.
My voice became the voice of a bear
With honey on my lips.
I was less myth and more despair.
My hooves became feet;
My horns flattened on my head.
I was recognized as a neighbor.
No one knows I lurk inside the
Roots of trees and write poetry
When the moonlight
Licks my chest as I raise my paw
To caress the darkness.

A WOMAN IN LOVE

Touch me there, and I will tell you why.
— Anonymous

Soften my breasts with your flat tongue.
Knead me into dough or dunes
Or into the shape of your desire.
Form a circle on my nipples with your lips.
Even use your teeth with little pressure.
If I turn my head to the side and swoon,
You will know you are ready to swallow me.
I will be your fruit. Peel me like an orange.
Suck the juice from my flesh.
Refresh your throat.

THE GRAVITY OF YOUR BODY

I can feel the light seeping into me slowly.
— **Anonymous**

The gravity of your body on my body
Melts into my skin, seeps into my chest,
Makes your skin lavender and silk.
When you place your breasts and legs
Onto my body, I feel the bond of sea glue,
Sun glue, a substance that merges my
Chest with your breasts, my lips to your lips.
We form a seal made of wax and passion.
We are pages placed together
Inside the book of our bed.

THE END OF THE AFFAIR

In the month of red leaves I climb to a bed of fire.
— Sylvia Plath

Say it. You desire my breasts and what you can extract
With your lips and tongue for your own pleasure.

Say it. You admit it is not love but the erosion of my skin
Onto your skin.

Say it. I trickle from the tea leaves of your lips
As you taste how well I am steeped inside you.

Say it. I am more spring to your flower
For the aroma of my petals to please you.

Say it. I am more flesh than kisses.

Say it. You'd rather unbutton my dress
Than plant geraniums with me.

Say it. You are more interested in the tunnels
Of my body than the excursions
Across my breasts and shoulders.

Say it. Your saliva is for your own lubrication
And not to mingle with the Nile in my mouth.

Say it. I am more nude caged in your lion's circus
Than dressed as a carousel for our delight.

Say it: lust at your lips; not love in your hands.

A WOMAN'S SUGGESTION

Heal me with your tongue.
        ---Anonymous

Make your choice about
The wound between my legs.
Do you wish to paddle inward,
Seeking alligators and herons?
Perhaps you wish
To rest inside me for a while
And feel what it is like
To be held between
My spasms and throbbing.
Do you wish to heal me?
Do you wish to sample
My interior liquid?
Perhaps you would like
To measure the wound
And prescribe your healing tongue.
If you'd like, you can spill
The ocean of yourself into me, or
Fertilize my garden with your seeds.
I promise that if you choose
To apply the salve of your lips
Onto me, you will hear
My healing moans
At the tip of my sleeping.

PLANTING

Men plant; women harvest.
-— Anonymous

I spill my body onto the ground
As a seed in spring.
I let the moisture seep into my skin.
I suck the earth of your body
While inhaling the minerals
Of your flesh until I begin to root.
I rummage between your breasts
For the best summer heat.
When my body
Is firmly rooted inside you,
My head breaks upward
From your rich soil
And I am newly born,
A marigold in autumn,
Resting inside your vase
Refreshed and satisfied.

TOUCH HAS MEMORY

Crossed over on the other shore
The lovers are edge to edge — Nicole Espagnol

I will touch you with the spikes of hard rain.
I will touch you with the fur of the lion.
I will touch you eagerly with oil on my hands.
I will touch you with the length of my tongue.
I will touch you with the stem of lilies.
I will touch you with the words in my poems.
I will touch you with our separate grieving.
I will touch you with a flat stone.
I will touch your forehead with my blessing.
I will touch you with my fever.
I will touch you with the tips of sea waves.
I will touch you with the ridges of a shell.
I will touch you as if you are made of feathers.
I will touch you with the sound of my breathing.
I will touch you until your skin swallows my fingers.
I will touch you with the moisture on my lips.
I will touch you while you are sleeping.
I will touch you when the moon undresses you.
I will touch you when your breasts heave upward.
I will touch you with the slant of the morning sun.
I will touch you with the dancers of Degas.
I will touch you with the paste of almonds.
I will touch you in April.
I will touch you with the smoke from Siam.
I will touch you the way bamboo is silent.
I will touch you edge to edge.

PART 7

I AM THE HYACINTHS OF YOUR DESIRE

I have a deeply hidden and
inarticulate desire for something
beyond the daily life. —Virginia Woolf

I am the hyacinths of your desire.
Claim my aroma for your pleasure.
My breasts are better than petals.
Caress the stem of my legs
And you will find the soil
At the tips of my roots.
I belong to my own garden.
Use the latch of your tongue
To open my gate.
Find me among the
Stains of dew on my skin.
I heard you know
The daffodils and
Their willing movement
Towards your lips. I am a choice.
Be the air on my breasts.
Infuse me with your aroma.
Unbutton your own petals.
Brush my pollen onto your legs.
Taste my nectar. Know who I am.

THE PEACH AND THE POET

We are meant to peal the fruit and swallow.
                            — Anonymous

Pick the fruit of me from
Beyond the edges of your body.
I am not an almond or sea bass.
I am ripe with juice in my veins
And oil on my skin.
You cannot reattach me to my stem.
Be my new stem, infuse me
With the sun and moisture
Of your desire. Call me a
New found peach with the blush
Of peach color on my cheek.
My breasts resemble a peach,
The color of spring and the texture
Under your tongue.
Please do not let the fur of my body
Touch the ground. I bruise easily.
I do not want to be a meal
For the coming bees.
Join me in my central path.
I was first a blossom and now
The ripe fruit. Your hand on my skin
Makes me feel more like a woman
Than a fruit. Let us find a place for love.
Let us believe we can make ourselves
More than flesh to eat and drink.
Here, this place, the grass is dry.
Stand before me. Let me open
The cloth between your legs
Like a book. Let me read your middle pages
As I unfold the words of your body
Extending towards my lips.
I repeat the words. I memorize the words.
I am eager for you to inject my fruit
With your words.
I am the peach and you are the poet.

EVEN WHEN YOU SLEEP

Even when you sleep I feed you.
                    — Ana Codjoe

I see your arm
Under your head as a pillow.
I am able to see
In the dark because of the
The moonlight dripping fruit from the
Space between the curtains.
When I touch your hand,
There is a slow motion
As your fingers curl inward.
We ran among the wolves.
We traded places
With the sea waves.
There is a movement of your legs
And a slight sound
Of the sheets moving.
I whisper the shape of your face.
I place my breast at your lips
And feel a soft sweetness.
Even when you sleep I feed you.

A WOMAN'S SUGGESTIONS

Excite my breasts
and patrol my vagrant heart.
　　　　— Jayne Cortez

Startle my breasts
With your tongue or eyes,
Both makes for a
Sudden purpose with my hands
On your chest.

Wander the lines
Of my lips with your lips.
Explore how they part
And trace the circles we create.

There is a fire in our mouths:
Rich wood; no place for charcoal.

Let us drink below
The timberline of our bodies,
Refresh our throats with the streams
Between our legs:
You the thick salmon and I
The silver liquid
Guiding us upstream.

EACH SPRING MIMICS A WOMAN

Spills the scent of her body over the thistle of the world
— Silvia Grénier

In my mouth I taste the reverence of your tongue,
A wave at the tip of any sea, rich with
Salt and movement.

I inhale the aroma of jonquils on your skin
As the moon bleeds between your legs.

There is the hint of incense spilling from
The green hills of spring
And the lightness of your breasts at my lips.

Within the walls of my desire
My liquid stones splash inside your body.
I am eager to unfold and stretch upward
Onto your breasts.

There are no wolves, just the sound of wolves,
A distant hunt for beauty
That spills onto the landscape of your arrival.

Nude, you run on the surfaces of the lake
Mimicking the swans with your arms open wide
As if ready to skim the surface of my body.

CONDITIONS FOR LOVE

*What a woman tells her lover in desire
should be written out on air & running water.*
— Catullus

To love, purge yourself first
From lust and roses,
Sleep upon my breast like a reclining star.
If you begin with just the taste of my lips,
You will end with infinite hunger,
But if you write my name in the air and on water,
Believe that I am mist and moisture,
If you seek my secret fire,
If you unspool the flower from between my legs
And tenderly plant yourself among the petals,
Then I will give you permission to love me
For then you will know how.

BUTTERFLY WOMAN

"I must have her, even though
I injure her butterfly wings. "
        — Pinkerton

Love submits to pain.
The body is rearranged.
The face smoothes into light.
Breasts become tense.
There is a new language
Forming on her lips.
If you grab the butterfly
With too much force,
She will collapse
Like a stale autumn leaf,
But if you caress her wings
Tenderly she will
Birth with fluid from the bulb
Of her chrysalis
And rise newly formed and settle on
The tip of your blossom and
Drink your nectar.

EXTRACTION

I have caught you. You are mine.
—from Madame Butterfly

What is hidden
Under the wings
Of the butterfly:
Breasts? Nectar? Pollen
Powered on her legs?
I watch her shadow
Covering the bud
Of my flower
As she extracts the
Liquid sun from my
Exposed blossom.

MARINER'S DREAM

The ocean is an open sex.
Whales and dolphins
Understand the way to
Penetrate the water
And slide inward
While holding their breath.
The skin of the ocean
Is perfumed with salt.
You can taste it on your lips
When you spread your body
On the beach while listening
To the tides moan
In rhythmic ecstasy.
Touch an ocean pearl
And feel the spasms of
Waves at your fingertips.
Swim among the anemones.
Feel the legs of her seagrass
Caressing your legs.
The ocean is feminine.
When you swim inside
Feel her embrace.
Tenderly use
Poseidon's spear to hold her
For a moment's pleasure
Until the currents
Of her body
Wash you back
To the dark shore
Of your bed.

BECAUSE OF ALL THINGS

Anyway. Just in case I forgot to mention it.
I love you. Did I get around to mentioning that?
                              —J.D. Salinger

I love you because of the pine sap on my palms.
I love you because of the spring aromas.
I love you because there are doves on the roof.
I love you because the horse is neighing.
I love you for the feel of a book in my hand.
I love you because of the taste of an orange.
I love you because of the shadows.
I love you because there are eggs in the spring nest.
I love you because I heard rumors about a carnival.
I love you because dolphins swim at night.
I love you because our skin is flexible.
I love you because the moon is fickle.
I love you because there is room for me beside you.
I love you because there are stones in the garden.
I love you because you dance the waltz.
I love you because of your dance shoes.
I love you because of Niagara Falls.
I love you because there is a crow in the oak tree.
I love you because the stars prink the darkness.
Because of all things, I love you.

PART 8

YOUR LOVE ALTERS
THE SHAPE OF MY BODY

If you do not feel the upward surge,
it is not love. **—Anonymous**

Your love alters the shapes of my breasts.
There is a swelling, the points of my nipples
Become chocolate or bits of marzipan
For your tongue; the hinges of my thighs loosen,
My lips become lined with moisture.

Do you see how the muscles in my face soften?
My skin may as well be the skin of a serpent
Coiling around your chest. When I spin before you
I become malleable, like potter's clay
On the wheel of your hands.
My hair becomes autumn wheat.
Even my hands become ferns to stroke your thighs.

Your love transforms my breathing to song.
My eyes become fire to burn my desire
Until I heat my hollow mouth with your
Flames of moving seeds.

Because of your love, I become water
Smoothing the stones in the stream bed of your body.

Because of your love,
I am formed with the impulse of two bodies merging:
The body that I am given, and my body arranged
With your hands, the only alteration that I seek.

YOU ARE BEAUTY AMONG THE EGRETS

We both hope that happiness
May also be like a white bird
Quietly descending —Lin Ling

Beauty is not heaven's gift.
It comes in the form of the lotus blossom.
It is on the backs of swans in the early mist.
When I see light at the edge of a window,
I think of the space between your open kimono.
When I see your sandals beside my shoes,
I watch how you caress the blanket of our bed.
Your beauty is hidden inside
The ocean shells where the sea whispers,
Where pearls lick each other.
Beauty is made of silk and rough sand,
The flat of my hand on your breasts.
Our lips break the origin of language
As I find new words that define your beauty:
When the air leans against the grass at dawn,
Beauty; when the reeds root into the moist soil,
Beauty; the egret on still wings, beauty.
You walking under the clouds of heaven.
You touching the earth with your hand.

HALF DREAM HALF FLESH

Souls and bodies should go together.
 — Louisa May Alcott

I obey the rules of nature.
There are borders to passion:
The edge of the sea is made for
Sand and picnics.
The murmur of clouds
Define spring.
The jade of your beauty
Is hard not soft.
Even the length of salmon
Defines what I can
And cannot do with your body.
Draw a line to the horizon,
And there you will find
How I write with a pen
When I think of you
From the lasting night to
Bits of dying dew.
If I loosen your sash,
And expect to see your breasts,
The fantasy is already ruined,
But holding you in the dark,
I am not blind to the beauty
Of your spring soul.
We live with restrictions.
A fox cannot love a bear.
Winter will not place his tongue
Into the mouth of spring.
The lotus blossom fits between your legs.
There is no other way to love you.
I touch the hem of your beauty,
And count the buttons on your dress.

EXPECTING HIS ARRIVAL

A woman in love consults the mirror.
                    — Anonymous

I will tell you a secret:
My dressing mirror is playful.
When she mimics my breasts
I believe there
Is liquid jade inside my body.
When I comb my hair, the mirror
Spills goldfish onto my feet.
The mirror is made of my glass skin.
If I turn, the mirror turns.
When I touch my face,
The mirror becomes coy.
When I touch my lips,
The mirror tells me I am ready
For my love's arrival
With the moon in his pocket.

EVENING RENDEZVOUS

Hear soft breathing outside your door,
And sense someone quietly near you.
— **Cheng Min**

If I touch the door
Without knocking,
Will you know that
I have come with
A rose from my garden?
I fear you will not hear
The sound of my breathing.
Perhaps I will ask the moon
To announce my arrival.
If it is only a door
That divides us, you will
Inhale the aroma of the rose.

THE SECRET MOON ON MY LIPS

The mass of men lead lives
of quiet desperation. —-**Henry David Thoreau**

I tried to leave the body of stars,
But the moon haunts me still.

I thought I could escape
The seduction of light inside my body,
But the edges of the moon caressed my lips.

I tried to drink silence into my mouth,
But the moon pulled the geese from the lake
And the cicadas complained about the light.

The disorder illuminated the garden flowers
With a gray light. I tried to avoid the deep center.
I tried to reassemble the stars and make
My own pictures, not bears and lions,
But women and egrets.

The ancient scribes called the moon an egret,
And women stirred the coals of the fire
As each ember rose and touched
The dark and spread wide instruction on forming
Ways to kiss the moon.

SPAWNED

I am spent. Do not touch me.
I am no longer a spike but a
Wounded salmon with the hook
Of your breast torn from
Mouth, and my skin returned to scales.
I am a beast again
With no hands to seduce you.
Feel my fins. I am made of slick skin
And silver eyes. When I was
Inside you, you reeled me in
Deeper than I expected. I felt
What I thought were my
Legs and arms when they were
Just the length of my compact body
Caught between your hands.
Your voice passed through my gills.
When you kissed me I resembled a man.
When you opened your eyes,
I slid out from between your thighs
And I swam back into the darkness
Among the sea grass and vanished using
The slow movement of my tail.

LET ME BE A TOURIST OF YOUR BODY

Sees Helen's beauty in a brow of Egypt:
— William Shakespeare

Let me be a tourist of your body,
My hand charting the map of your skin.
I am eager to explore the
Pharaoh's tomb between your thighs
Where gold bliss and hieroglyphs
Wait for my tongue and for
Our interpretations.
I'd like to mount the camels of
Your breasts and extend my reach
Towards the oasis of your mouth:
Moist and good for drinking.
The guide says I must reserve a spot
To climb the pyramid of your hips,
So while I wait I will listen to the Nile
Flowing inside me ready to find its way
To the lips of your Mediterranean.

LOVERS ONCE ON THE FADING GRASS

Youth is once in a single time. —Anonymous

I have been to the side of the moon,
An exclusive visit where apple trees grew and
And a boy swam nude with mud on his back
And with a daisy in his hair
As the girl waited on the grass for
The boy to return with his story
About how a salmon tickled his legs
And he asked the girl "Can I kiss you like a daisy?"
And the girl said that she is all stem and petals
As she opened like a fresh blossom.
And the moon leaned closer to the earth,
And the earth swallowed the moon,
And the boy and girl swooned and lost themselves
In what they didn't know would vanish:
The light to their moon; and the earth of their bodies
As the moon returned to the night,
And the earth began to spin again
As the boy and the girl grew old in the fading light
And no one remembered except the grass and the salmon.

I CAN PROTECT YOU

*I did not know when you were born
the aroma of spring was your first breath.*
                        —-Anonymous

I want to protect you. Watch the sea
And how it protects the shells.
I know how to touch
The tender pearls of your body.
The tides of my body match
The tides of your body.
Your mouth is a whirlpool for my kisses.
Let me make stares
With the coral of your skin.
The currents inside my body are eager
To discharge on your breasts.
Let my hand swim downward
Like an eel as I undress you,
As if we are going to die in pleasure.
I will not trick your beauty.
We did not meet by chance.
I watched your lips from a distance.
I learned that dolphins do not breathe
Without your dreaming.
I am your secret foam
At the edge of your open sea.
I can bathe you confidently.
I can love you with kisses and starfish
On top of the ocean of your breasts.
I can use my tongue to
Dream inside your mouth.
I can protect you.
You are not a fragile illusion.
You are what makes the
Spring jealous.

PART 9

ANAÏS NIN TO HENRY MILLAR

How wrong is it for a woman to expect
the man to build the world she wants,
rather than to create it herself?
— Anaïs Nin

You do not need my body.
My wound is privately alive.
I do not need tentacles entering me,
Or wet roots. I am my own sea creature,
My own blossom. I have given enough
Of my false self for your pleasure.

Find something warm to touch,
Not just my breasts or thighs.

Why should I wait for pleasure?
Why not hang under the horse of your chest
And feel the movement as we
Gallop towards the open field
Of our private bed?

I am either a woman or a poem.
Decide what you want written on your skin.

Take all that you want that I cannot give.
There lies the passion.

If you think of me as a myth, you will not notice
My breasts are uneven.

Drain my strength and I will swallow you
Until I find where I begin.

I have arranged my body alone for you,
Prepared each fold, manicured my nails,
Arranged my hair in curls
So that you do not recognize me,
So that you will not remember my face.
I want to give you this unattached pleasure.

I am ruthless with my desires. You will
Feel my claws tearing at your flesh
As if I am a wolf
And you are the warm carcass of
A buck with blood streaming onto your fur,
Down your legs, draining what makes you a man.

When you see me undress,
Will you take pleasure with my skin again?
Do you remember which of my nipples is
More sensitive than the other?
Will you remember what I like best:
The looking first and then your words of gratitude?

You are not a magician
Ready to transform who I am into a
Woman ready to be cut in half with your single blade.
I swallow your wand.
I come to you with a new language.
I want you to observe the movement of my arms
And legs and how they seem to
Weave onto your body like fast growing ferns.

I am loyal to my body. I do not allow harm.
I expect a seduction with familiar things:
Your lips, your eyes, your words
Explaining why you want to divide my legs
And hunt for feathers or shells.
I am made of feathers and shells.
There is no other substance.

I do not wear a disguise. My clothes on the floor
Are bits of leaves and bark.

You must be obedient to my body.
Follow the spasms. Erect yourself
Bedside me with tenderness.

Taste me twice with your two tongues.

WHERE TO PLACE A POEM

A poet looks at the world the way
a man looks at a woman. —Wallace Stevens

Let me place this poem on your lap
And pretend it is my hand
As I ask you to feel the movement of
Blood and desire in my fingers.
I try to turn words into my flesh.
Letters have a sound when laced together,
The same way you murmur when we
Join the syllables of our bodies
And we create a new poem.
Do you feel the hints of meaning
When I unbutton your blouse?
Do you see the length of words when I
Undress and seek your question mark
As I use my exclamation point?
Some poems rhyme making a similar sound
Like the sound you make when
I caress your breasts.
Some poems have rhythm
Similar to the movements we make
When we rock into each other
Like my hand rising and falling as I read
The poetry of you, as I open the
Pages of your lap.

HOW I WRITE A POEM

A woman is a poem. —Khalil Gibran

With the muse
I start with the smooth
Defiance of skin
When permission is granted
To open her clothes
And seek the almonds
Of her breasts.
I slowly tangle my hands
Inside the coral
Of her arms and legs.
There is always honey
At the center of her rose,
Always immense nudity,
A purpose to pursue beauty
With the poem.
She is a cascade
Of water on my chest,
The tongue of the muse
Splashing on my pen;
The paper always smooth,
My ink always wet.

POETRY DEFINED

Poetry is what seeps from our loins.
                    — Anonymous

Poetry? Ask the swans to dance.
Expect words that breathe.
Believe a rose is evidence of life.

Poetry? Hidden beneath,
The surface of an orange,
Untying pleasure,
Little myths about dying,
A logical caress,
Dancing with flowers.

Poetry? The poverty of tongues,
A quarrel with passion,
A habit to lick.

Poetry escapes into shadows,
Feels love without knowing,
And is hungry for a caress.

Poetry? The tip of your breast,
The taste of snow,
The backs of salmon,
Dangling lilacs of men,
Winter sheets of women.

Poetry? Holy oil on your forehead.

A WOMAN'S CONFIDENCE WITH LOVE

It is forbidden to love where we are not loved.
                    — Sharon Olds

With one kiss you will know who I am, not
My public self with pressed clothes and a smile.
Adjust your hips to lock against my hips.
We can roll in the sea like sea turtles mating.

When you taste the water of my breasts
You will understand my need
To float on my back and long for the tentacles
Of your body to probe the open shell of my body.

You can cut all the flowers and still you will not find
The April of my nectar, my pollen will not
Brush against you unless you believe
In the taste of my honey.

Love is not a random gesture: a poke, a prick,
Or the movement of your hands on my breast.
Love is moving my shoes to the side of the bed
So that I can find them at dawn.
Love knows how to caress the easy sides of my thighs.
When you touch me, there ought to be
Doves in the room, or the sound of doves
From my throat cooing.

I have found the answer for those who arrive
With coconut oil in a bottle.
Watch how I use my hand as I apply the oil onto your skin.
Feel how I massage the sorrows from your arms and legs.

I like to watch how you open your mouth when I
Caress the sudden expansion of your malleable stone.

This is love. We are meant to wear out our lips.
Love is meant for exhaustion. Measure my love
With the taste of my breasts in your mouth.
Watch me rise in a plume of flesh and merriment.

I like the way that you lie under me.
I am coconut oil.

GOOD MORNING

Morning without you is a dwindled dawn.
    — Emily Dickinson

I search for you each morning.
When I open the horizon I see
Your light is the light of dawn.
When I touch the grass
It is as if I feel the dew of your
Breasts on my cheek.
When I welcome the flowers they
Lean forward and whisper your name.
The morning is for greeting
The arrival of your memory.
I bathe to remember what it is like
To feel you rising on my skin:
The warmth of your lips on my lips,
The rays of your hands on my face.
I dress each morning.
I unbutton your breasts on my chest.
I slip the sleeves of my arms
Inside your arms. I insert my legs
Inside the length of your legs.
This is how I prepare each day.
Good morning.

FIRST LOVE THEN SEX

I love you like this because
I don't know any other way to love.
          — **Pablo Neruda**

I am a man.
You can tell beyond
The fruit dangling
Between my thighs.
I am worth more than
A taste in your mouth.
I am more than an orange
To peel for your pleasure.
I understand your caution.
Men like to explore,
Push their ships
Onto the sea of your body,
Enter caves with a
Stick and paint
Their images on your breasts.
Men like fire.
I understand that I can
Easily disappoint you
When I offer you
Only the sap from my wood
And not the entire forest.
Forgive me.
When I ask you to drink
My nectar, I will first
Cover you with petals of kisses.

YOU ARE THE FIELD OF LAVENDER

But one man loved the pilgrim soul in you,
And loved the sorrows of your changing face;
— William Butler Yeats

I have been to the field of lavender,
And inhaled the memory of you.
Do you remember how the lake felt
When you stepped into the water?
Was it like my hands on your breasts,
Or the feeling of summer?
Now that we have curled ourselves
Inside the petals of the rose,
Do you remember the taste of nectar?
There was a time when you undressed me
As I was dressed in dew,
And you licked the moisture from my skin.
When we first met I watched you dance
And said how much like a swan you were.
Now that the fields are fallow,
And the lake a forgotten postcard,
Now that autumn
Are dried leaves on your breasts,
And the rose is only a poem;
Now that we drink tea and not nectar,
And the dew is just what happens at dawn,
I still wish to watch you dance
In the field of blue lavender.

WE TWO BECOME A POSSIBILITY

When you look at me, in our most intimate
exchanges, you drape my nakedness
in a fabric I neither sewed nor bought.
— Ama Codjoe

Your eyes sew desire on my breasts.
You drape my nudity with the fabric of your hands.
I am lined with my dress for your unraveling.
My buttons are keys to unlock.
I am opulent in your eyes: the silk of my skin,
My eyes, amethyst imported from your dreams.
We can exchange skin to skin
As swallows intersecting in their flight.
We can be pollen and nectar combined
To form the amber nudity of honey.
I do not flee from the obvious.
I am not hidden inside the tip of my stem.
I do not fear the opening of
My blossom, the petals of my arms and legs
Presenting my truth for your delight.
If we remove the distance,
The skin of your hand becomes
The skin of my breasts.
We can discover our second bodies
As we blend the earth and root of you
With the sea and canyons of me.
My tongue can become your language.
Your mouth can swallow my words.
Let us be nude in the air of ourselves
Floating as invisible dust.
Seeking a surface to complete our movements.
All begins in nudity; all ends in nudity.
In between we dress for fashion, modesty,
Or shame, or even for protection.
Begin with my face exposed. Interpret my eyes,
And when you are certain I am ready
For the dew from your mouth,
Embroidered my body with your lips.

REUNION

Is it possible I will touch you
As real as a summer rose?

Is it possible I will inhale your aroma?
If I kiss you, will you
Not disappear into my desire?

When we meet, do I say your name,
Or would you prefer
Silence and my tongue?

We could stand apart for a moment
And pretend that we are strangers,
And laugh when the spell is broken.

When we fill the space between us
With our first embrace, will we be able
To unwind and rearrange our skin,
Trying to decide which is yours
And which is mine?

There is no place I'd rather be then
In our first embrace, when lost time
Is forgotten and we once again mingle
Face to face.

PART 10

I AM A WOMAN. YOU
CANNOT POSSESS ME

*No one worth possessing
can quite be possessed.*
          — Sara Teasdale

You cannot possess me
Or even identify me as a woman.
I am all stone and sea kelp.
I am any sort of tern or feathered lust
As easy as a saw to the tree,
As common as a coffin to the dirt.
Possess me and I revolt.
I will spill my breasts
Not onto your lips but onto
Your fading shadow
And refuse to release
What is moist inside my body.
Look for me in the
Crease of my palms.
Know where my hands have been:
Planting roses,
Measuring the chest of men,
Finding my own pleasure
Between the spark of my thighs.
Watch me ignite and see the way
I mimic the movement of your hand:
Crisp and secure
On the surface of my skin.
To own me is to excavate my secret place:
Where I sucked the nectar from
From the tips of honeysuckle,
Where I first found the word fuck inside
A book of poems in my father's shelves,
The explanation my mother gave when
I showed her blood on my fingertips.
I did not want to be a woman yet.
I was a gardener making roses
With pipe cleaners and pink felt.
Do you think you can possess my thoughts?

A foolish idea.
If I think about my breasts, will you wear them
As medallions on your chest?
If I think about elephants, will you
Spray your back with dust or water?
If you bleed me of myself,
Purge the sorrows of my joy,
Even then you will not know who I am.
You will not tie me to your tongue
Or to your meaning.
I know the names of stars and the way
The evening spills over my lips.
If you mimic the stars,
If you mimic the evening,
If you touch the stars to my breasts
And caress me with the evening felt,
Then, perhaps, you may have me
Until dawn.

MY IMAGE DOES NOT SWOON AT YOUR TOUCH

A photograph will not kiss you back. —Anonymous

What do you want? Do you want to just look at me
And see how the shadows and bits of light caress my breast?
Is that all you want, to ogle without knowing my name?
When you touch my photograph,
Do you feel the softness of my skin?
Do you think there is blood in my veins?
It is a pity men are not interested in arms and shoulders.
I like being caressed on my arms and shoulders.
I like that kind of a man.
Look at my face. Do you see sternness?
Do you see Passion?
Do you know that I am thinking it is winter
And I will need a better blanket at night to keep warm?
What are you going to do with my image?
Hang it on the wall of your desire? Refer to it
When you wish to extract your lava in a rhythmic flow?
A picture is a flat outline, never the taste of my lips.

I CAN BE YOUR TRAVEL AGENT

We are but made of maps and postcards.
                    — Anonymous

Climb down into my body.
Explore my folds and creases.
When you find something appealing,
When you arrive, use your eyes first
To decide what you want to see.
I am flexible.
If you wish to examine my eyes,
Look how the iris opens and closes
In the light and half light.
You will need to learn
How I speak with my eyes
If you wish to make the full discovery.
It might help to use my skin as a map.
It might help to plot your journey
In order to touch my best topography.
I can guide your hand if you'd like,
Point out the best place to touch my breast,
Or the easy way to balance yourself
Between my thighs.
Think of my body as an adventure
With hidden storms and ocean spasms.
I can be your travel agent.

YOU ARE THE POEM

A woman easily becomes a poem.
                    — Anonymous

I am glad to see you again.
You are poetry, not prose.
I recapture the scent of your skin
And reject the bizarre air
That separated us.

The only form of suffering
Resides in my empty hands.

Because you do not exist
When you are away, I invent you,
I breathe you into poetry.
I massage your image
In my lost passion.

Now that you are here
Beside me once more, I am swollen
With the poems of you.

The words of my sorrow
Are saved on my palms that I print
With my hands on your breasts
As I recite my longing
With my lips on your lips
As we exchange the continued draft
Of this poetry anthology.

WHEN DOES A MAN STOP WRITING ABOUT WOMEN

I can only fasten down with this work of my hands
these painfully assembled stones —Adrienne Rich

When does a man stop writing about women?
When China discovers pandas prefer eating
Moonlight rather than bamboo,
When the ocean spits our flowers instead of shells?

There are secrets hidden inside words, and words are feminine
Dressing and undressing, deciding when to be sensual, and overt.
If men stop writing about the galaxy of women,
The stars will crumble to sand in our hands,
No more constellations, no more bears and dragons
Tearing at our flesh with desire.

Women contain unwritten novels and poems.
They float egrets in the air of their dreaming.
They use their hands to guide the pen of any man who believes
Without women there is no poetry.

Men wilt without women. Men do not know how to
Match order with passion.

If you believe women are myths with breasts
And with laurel in their hair, you will not be a poet.
Men who dream that women are nymphs
And cushions are not writing, they are rubbing
The flesh of woman onto their own bodies
For their own pleasure. That is not writing, that is erosion.

When a man stops writing about women,
The color of the sun is black, the taste of a peach
Becomes a stale fish, his writing becomes
Masculine, hard; the earth of his writing is filled with sand
And not with oil.

Men stop writing about women when they forget
The tongue of tenderness in their words.

AUTHOR PROFILE

Christopher de Vinck, a husband, father, and grandfather, earned his doctoral degree from Columbia University and devoted 40 years to his career in public education. This is his 20th book. His previous books have been published by HarperCollins, Doubleday, MacMillan, Hodder, Crossroads, Paulist Loyola, and Upper Room.

Over 200 of Christopher's op/ed essays have been published in: *Readers Digest Wall Street Journal, ,The Pittsburgh Post-Gazette, The NJ Record, The Dallas Morning News, The National Catholic Reporter, The Chicago Tribune Good Housekeeping and USA Today, The   New   York Times,*

Christopher is a contributing columnist for *The Dallas Morning News.* He is author of Ashes (HarperCollins); Mr. Nicholas (Paraclete Press); The Power of the Powerless (Hodderz) (Doubleday) Augusta & Trab (Macmillan); (HaperCollins) (Crossroad Books)

www.ingramcontent.com/pod-product-compliance
Lightning Source LLC
Chambersburg PA
CBHW070502170726
48291CB00008B/2613